I0610689

GLITCHES IN THE FBI

GLITCHES IN THE FBI

AMARIS FELAND KETCHAM

Casa Urraca Press

ABIQUIU

Cover design by Amaris Feland Ketcham.
Set in Helvetica and Garamond No. 8.

First edition, v. 1.1

ISBN 978-1-7351516-1-8

CASA URRACA PRESS

an imprint of Casa Urraca, Ltd.
PO Box 1119
Abiquiu, New Mexico 87510
casaurracaltd.com

To Andy
& all
the stargazers

CONTENTS

AUTHOR'S NOTE

original dialogue

Rainy nights, with a flashlight cutting through the forest; long shadows down narrow hallways flanked in darkness; improbably, even the basements of the FBI building seemed foggy—these were the scenes that I loved watching when *The X-Files* aired in the 1990s. I spent many Friday nights immersed in its eerie atmosphere and fantastical stories. It was only recently while re-watching some episodes that I came to appreciate the dialogue, and out of a playful impulse, started to experiment with lines from the script.

The poems in *Glitches in the FBI* are composed of lines of dialogue re-purposed from *X-Files* episodes. While each poem contains words that may reference *The X-Files*, they don't rely on the TV show, individual episodes, or prior knowledge to be enjoyed. These poems are an experiment in mixing found poetry and fan fiction poetry. Found poetry is a type of literary collage, where words or phrases are taken from an original source and placed in a new context to be read as poetry. This re-framing of the original material has a long history, often employed by the Dadaists and Surrealists to challenge our concept of authorship, spark creativity, and revise drafts of works in progress. Unlike fan fiction, which appropriates characters and storylines, these poems describe neither what happens on *The X-Files*, nor who the characters are. Therefore, approaching them with an expectation that they will recreate or reinvent an episode would only hinder one's reading.

I reference the episodes for further enjoyment for those who wish to revisit them. While the episode might provide the "occasion" for the poem, I strove to write away from the source material so each poem became something new. Often, something small that was mentioned only in passing would inspire a poem—a "trigger," as the poet Richard Hugo would call it. I made a variety of rules for myself while writing, such as never using more than two words in a row from the original source, but like most rules, these were occasionally broken. However, the poems are still indebted to the writers of the show for frequently using such interesting and precise words. The poems retain a similar sense of mystery and inquiry, mirroring and adapting big ideas and issues, and a smattering of references and slang that make them read like a kind of 1990s Homeric.

GLITCHES IN THE FBI

I WANT TO BELIEVE

repurposed dialogue from Season 1, Episode 8

Loud and clear
solar winds blow across
a trick of light and shadows,
minus three seconds.

So you think this X-ray is bogus?
Lock your visors deep.

How do you read a comeback
like winged astronauts
knowing something might go wrong
in a rusty old bucket?

Can you trace
T-minus an accident?

I'm breaking up.
I'm standing by, cutting
off a dull thump,
your boyhood hero.

Houston? You take care.
Beyond reentry, it's anybody's guess.

THE SURVIVOR PRONOUNCES

repurposed dialogue from Season 1, Episode 14

Whenever I look up at the stars—
the tunnel, the light, people rising up
and viewing their own bodies,
this kooky electrical overload—
I know that Lula's looking at the same ones.

Cells die and genetic material unfolds,
releasing this tremendous charge of energy
in every near-death experience.

I can't wear a watch now.
Not with this zest for life.

Everything I see, I see her.
Each brilliant aura or temporal load,
in the print kit, the EKG strip,
first and last month's rent, cash.

A buck knife sliced open my palm, her palm;
blood into the ocean, dividing
the grid of that long, black tunnel.

Two heartbeats died there tonight.
We resuscitated a body, which man came back
to the same dive, that slanting pool table—

What the hell?
She's such a creature of habit.

ATLANTIC CITY

repurposed dialogue from Season 1, Episode 4

I'm horning in on a myth:
are you more afraid of the gateway
to the galaxy or Jersey?

Anti-gravity holds me easy,
light as swearing to God.
But our dual nature
wilds the creature.

I knew a man.

A kind of bent folktale:
Bingo was his name-o,
or something he said again and
again swearing in a check-out
line to the drunk tank.

Man was a natural radar,
as jungled as myself,
unbelievable as night.

Now languageless and tribeless.
Don't mistake him
for a discovery, outside the realm
of luck crawled loose.

Fifty-fifty top carnivore
and Cirque du Soleil: human.
Another vagrant
millions of years out of Africa.

ORDINARY ANTI-WALTONS

repurposed dialogue from Season 1, Episode 2

Do little green men ever wake
from a deep sleep
read the newspaper and say
screw it? Climb the ladder
just to fall on their ass?
Do they open their minds
only to let somebody mess with their heads?
Do little green men ever get carried away
feel spooky or special, like they nailed it
or down and out and busted?
I wonder what it means to be down-to-earth
in another galaxy, leaving
a bizarre fingerprint on another history
searching for a close encounter,
any kind of message
to make you feel
like you've crawled out
of a nest and you're still safe
and awake for the first time?

CHASING SHADOWS

repurposed dialogue from Season 1, Episode 5

My mystery accomplices are all my goodbyes
trying to outrun reminders like the smell of aftershave
or the ridiculousness of saying "afterlife."
All these afters leave me with Liberty
Bell-sized headaches, where I want to break free
through the big crack. Give me a boost
and maybe I'll escape the want that you're watching
over me, that I'm too unaware to observe
spectral phenomena. Ever put something to rest
only to see it levitate? Say "poltergeist" and I think
"how Carrie got even at the prom." Say guide me
dancing, let me glow a little, the last person
you're leaving—two sufferings—and I
can only wish you luck, say goodbye.

TIME LOSS

repurposed dialogue from Season 1, Episode 10

I'd imagined in vitro fertilization
would be like getting abducted
like lying inside light
while aliens played doctor
they're knowledgeable strangers
maybe there's red lightning
in my uterus and outside
it's raining but I feel safe
I imagined naming the child
after the clouds
but instead it's very dark
and I only have this little flashlight.

RV GYPSY'S SINGULAR PASSION

repurposed dialogue from Season 1, Episode 9

Canyon night repeats across
ridges and county roads.
I see crop circles in the stars.
My fool's attention to speculation.

The last whoa ejected like firepower:

trust no one, Mother. At another ground
zero: animal one second,
then X-ray. At what frequency
do falcons ionize? 200,000 Mhz?

Aircraft, electronic fences, meteors, fallen
angels: 7,087 man-made objects in orbit.

Space is full
of aberrant movement.

Mother, how we echo.

HOWLING MAKES YOU STRONGER

repurposed dialogue from Season 1, Episode 3

Summer centered in the frame
of an Instamatic: the prom queen's heartache

hangs like a lightning strike in the middle of night.
Her sweetheart blisters like a sunburn

bright ruby, light lies
come weightlessness, come crying.

Momma won't you run howling
at the moon, on the sands of Lake Okoboji?

The way they threw stones at satellites
ranging sky-high, longshots all. Kids playing

and waiting for something to solidify
like the cryptography of their bodies.

At the campsite, the prom queen's sorry
she'd like to be rescued. With some rituals

an active imagination, and a little bundt cake
she'll leave the glass of night as it hangs

in the still lake and dive through
this fringe of storm clouds.

RED BIRD

repurposed dialogue from Season 1, Episode 1

pure stealth and wing-shake
an airshow drops from the clouds
they raid the bouquets

smelling of honey
at the edge of the tall weeds
memory lapses

these blurry photos
of hummingbirds hovering
in Russian airspace

PRAYING MANTIS EPIPHANY

repurposed dialogue from Season 3, Episode 12

Rumor molts, gently
blowing air, very hush-hush
in widespread reports.
Nowadays we're anti-Darwinian.

We are gods freaked
by the natural world,
by mystery. Give us a beer
and a motel room

something to watch at night
a road map to the outskirts
of self-illumination

so we can pry it off
like an old exoskeleton.

HE THINKS
HE'S PSYCHIC

repurposed dialogue from Season 3, Episode 4

If the future is written,
meaningful patterns interpreted
after the fact, a given
suggestion of images,
a whole series of tea leaves—

If the future is a choice,
modern myths in malt scotch
harboring one night in percentages,
crystal balls and spooky dolls—

If the future is an attitude,
lotto players, another strand of that silk,
a bellhop's intuition,
Miss Manners unlimited—

If the future is undignified,
Chantilly lace with coconut cream,
a better dancer than my last date,
a fat, white psychic—

—maybe he's lucky, but why
these chills, which is which:
Buddy Holly or the day the future dies?

TWELVE IN THE WORLD

repurposed dialogue from Season 3, Episode 11

High stigmatics   hell-bent on fabric winds;
so-called ones   changing bandages;
mutants with bald hands
interpreted   feverish,
on the playground,
like narrow altar boys   arrested

locked in division
signs step by step
by step waving;

long distance stigmatics letting go;

waking   can't remember, draw a bath;

townsfolk stigmatics
smell of flowers with barbs,
kitchens and carved animals   born partially;

formal stigmatics   bleeding again.

FLYING SAUCERS IN THE SECOND COMING

repurposed dialogue from Season 1, Pilot Episode

Every day's like Halloween here: unconventional
                    wisdom, unsupportable evidence, unidentified
          lights so bright you blink
          and theories disappear. Unsee

the FBI's most unwanted losing power, nine minutes,
                    brainwaves unsticking
          universal invariants from the far
          unreaches of space. Unrepressable

memories of campfires in the unwarm summers of Oregon,
                    the class of '89 uncelebrating
          unexplained phenomena and the spookiness
          of Einstein's Twin Paradox unable

to grasp reality, these wholly unsupportable regression hypnoses.
                    Here they wake unticking
          the fantastic one doubt
          at a time, undigging graves of unscientific

thinking until punctures through memories leave them unbound.

THE ROSE AGE

repurposed dialogue from Season 1, Episode 20

The world of druids
walking hills
clearing their heads
while elkhounds match their step,
bury trophies at their shoes.

The world a ripe green
constructive energy
placing stones upright.
Is it pretty? What
open minds.

The world a thousand eyes
peeking. People, animals,
pines trusting darkness
and vague hunches. Look,
a moose, a window
to his thoughts.

The world of druids sneaking
to the storage room, squeezing
honey late at night. So coppery.
Everyone's in bed. Only
the moose watching.

The world of fate
mapped like a rose
locked, druids' lives remained
framed as secrets.

THE TEXTURE OF ALL CLEAR

repurposed dialogue from Season 4, Episode 20

May the Force relax you
like a striated song from the stars:

He loves me. He loves me not.

Who knew obvious confessions
came from vestigial wars, bulbed
in memories, slipped into china patterns?
One day, we'll all be living
in trailer parks in space. Miles
of uniform buildings, born of wishes
to walk out the door, off the planet.

He loves me. An intersection.
Or not. Cold-cocked.
Breathe, planet-walker.

You have such spry fingerprints.
You're A-okay, counting chance
on the direction of winds.
It's now or never; it's not.

ONLY A CAT
CAN WORRY
ANCESTRAL RATS

repurposed dialogue from Season 3, Episode 6

Mona knows the superstitions
of old systems, the nature
and depth of bureaucracy.

She's feeling squirrely of late
about these artifacts
and their mythologies. History handcuffs

us, she says, projects security
while claiming our spirits. Form
letters should be buried in urns

along with free advice—so far
underground a thousand years
of tunnels won't excavate them.

Wild their whereabouts
and overflow them with curses,
Mona. If you save the bones

intact, it'll just doctor itself
summon determination and crawl
through the sewer with ceremony.

So let's hold in us a jaguar spirit,
give it some room for a personal jungle,
ready to take a thousand small bites.

SCHOOLBOY'S NEW AGE IDEAS

repurposed dialogue from Season 2, Episode 10

Hey, little brother, hey buttcrumb, don't get the creeps
when I talk about soul transference and the Age of Aquarius.
It's just this pepperoni pizza's a blessing of the dawning
of a new age, when we can be holy, delivered
from this monument to barbarism. Piss off all
those keepers of scorecards; that dog-eat-dog spite
will stick out like a sore thumb. What's this?
You're just getting motion sickness
from enlightenment. Like don't have a dairy cow,
mankind. I'm not ribbing you. I wouldn't
Nixon you. Tainted pastures beget tainted pastures.
Give it some earth years and this will make sense.
Kinda like we're animal spirits kept as pets
and bearing witness to a standstill between home
and the magic of morning light.

CROSSTOWN LINES

repurposed dialogue from Season 3, Episode 6

Poems as personal
           as the crosstown bus
brief looks or rudenesses
           the usual suspects
bump, break, grab, want, wake
           here's the morning paper
a column on hunger
           a grocery list
girls with essential oils, long fingernails
           don't need the hots for a future Mr. Right
not some vampire
           sucking their shine away
comb, knock, deal, fool, find, feel
           a habit like a lock
a suitcase of chances and lonelinesses
           next stop, get off
which way to the library?
           a handful of lines,
Bartlett's Quotations, texts
           this is her signature
jiving wishes, questions reading
           like four-leafed clovers

TIME FOR THAT TETANUS BOOSTER

repurposed dialogue from Season 2, Episode 2

We used to test the water
dip our ankles in
gather eggs, grab at snakes
play in the field after
talking about monsters.
Heavy rainfall
made the sewers overflow
into our waterway
raw, bizarre, discolored
not like real water
whatever the village flushed
into the smelly underground
catacombs. We called it
Chernobyl and told lies
about giant flukes who drew fools
down there, made you eat
"bupkis" and brush your teeth
with sewage: scrub, scrub, scrub
all with a smile. Think of the taste!
This could be Jersey, the sea
a radioactive soup, nature
mottled by adults—the way
the young warn one another,
the shape of a life cycle.

FOLKSTONE

repurposed dialogue from Season 2, Episode 15

Enough heavy dreaming and tales of impact.
At a crossroads, saying uncool *mercis*
and fighting back with nasty looks; shame
hangs from your shoulders like a broken peony.
Enough grave processing
of the true self. Loosen a little hell. Raise
the dead, then snatch their stories.
Graffiti freedom on every belief you see.

Flip failure: it's efficiency, even
charming. A crack in the sidewalk. A mirror
dug out of the sandbox. The easy magic
of a pair of fuzzy dice. The Statue of Liberty: the light
in her eyes. No voodoo can save you
from the country's amnesia. Enough

self-inflicted rituals. Freedom's a sacred trick,
confined before known.

FOXFIRE SPIRIT

repurposed dialogue from Season 2, Episode 24

Leaving town was just a formality.
Good people chasing some sweet young
superstition. Most legends don't leave
behind hang-ups and turn-offs.

Push comes to shove, and the whole town
welcomes a new story about hill people
massacres, swamp gas in the field,
scorched remnants of spirits.

Like some high-speed repetitive activity
layabouts ward off determination. Man is a line
hypnosis. Troublemakers cling tight
witch pegs in their hands and folly stuffing

their pillows at night. Some men build towns
some just chop away at them until the bonfire's
burned down and the faith once fed on ritual alone
passes through the spongelike holes in our stories.

SKYLAND INCOMPLETE

repurposed dialogue from Season 2, Episode 6

Because one man's dream, unmarked
serial truths spin: I, she, no one

deny everything. One truth, two, three truths, four
all implausible, damning. Because on the radio, there's a story

about sleeplessness in Chernobyl, Exxon Valdez,
Three Mile Island, in 190,000 fatal car crashes,

dozing linked to deaths or dreams or abductions or—
go back to the place where it all started

exit through the mountain sleep
ascending to the stars. Up and up

whistling "Stairway to Heaven."
Ship or unmarked helicopter—just a voice, a she,

no one, a dreamwork disconnecting,
awake when you want to slow down.

7:35 P.M. IS NOW SENTIENT

repurposed dialogue from Season 1, Episode 6

Never-minding my casual dark side,
I glimpsed a life of electro-travelers
these techno anarchists with no handle
on reality, all surface. Down at the warehouse
rounded clear, shared coaxing. I swore
on a holy sound bite and two Eastern Standard Time
evils. 7:35 taps the computer in trick-or-treats,
surges: Like an unstable, organic wound I tried
to quit reaching panic. Face flushed. Authority
is made more unwitting on a lone channel
hacked, our delusions decoded—
listen: a cherry new tone
traced as a Trojan and stacked
as an executed voice,
the wizardry of growing up

of owning mistakes—another alibi
but my jimmied soul, finally listening,
saying time is a booby trap, back out.

ASH IN THE WINE

repurposed dialogue from Season 2, Episode 7

In Malibu Canyon big-haired preachers
and other nobodies

talk about weird scenes. Exposure
freaks at corporate parties. You thought

red wine always looked purple
the way it stained your lips. The myth

of this city—the sun comes up,
no one atones; there's a mirror

for every indulgence—burns
quicker with each change

in the wind. You wish you could finish

like an old coroner's trick.
But damn, you're always breaking light.

IT'S RUSH HOUR ON TABLOID TV

repurposed dialogue from Season 3, Episode 22

Like our attention spans on the brink
our bitter fairy tales are going extinct
slued by the wailing of another afternoon talk
show. Straight from earthly confines, here be Loch
Ness and other monsters, National Geographic's pseudo-
anomalies, prehistoric ramblings, and collective crypto-
fears, forgotten. Mystery's endangered, knows how to hide.
Perched in some mental cove, snapping once you're outside.
Seek and ye shall find your unknown. Track
these happy obsessions. But don't turn your back
when undoing neckties and opening doors of perception.
Out of the big blue comes another question
about cosmology and cults, then folktales unzipping
speculation from warped significance, nipping
at a discovery once drowned in TV currents
before you heard the sound of your sea serpents.

SAVE FOR A MORE COSMIC SEASON

repurposed dialogue from Season 2, Episode 18

Centuries of elephant graveyards disappearing
in one sonic string with a whiff of animal.

Here a boom of spines, seashells crushed.
Night vision passing in a season, cutting

the protective custody of astrological fog.
Slow down, David Copperfield; shake

these unmistakable locks and tamper
with these tie-downs, never a worse time to be

withdrawn. In environments like thunder
holes, a life buffed behind bars:

faintly humane connections.

Craven thinking trapped in trouble
with the space-time continuum. All talk.

Heading back, oblivion follows
our odor in the wind.

WITNESS

repurposed dialogue from Season 1, Episode 15

When he died I thought I saw a fox
slipping through the field, lone

and clever. He ran in the country
like a ghost daring me

to blink. Blink and the haiku's over
blink and you forget

his eyes, the way he moves.
What came first, the chicken

or his coop, the promise
or the pressure? I trace

the pen grooves from his last note,
his handwriting clumsy with age.

The fox, too, is a right-hander
stepping out of the lot like a secret

feet afire, disguised in wooded land
but I've a hunch he's still out there

thriving and toothed and hidden
like a fluid cursive writing on.

MEN IN BLACK

repurposed dialogue from Season 3, Episode 20

Weird how forgettable it is that we are eyewitnesses
to the universe.

Venus in the sky
a brilliant light
drifting.

So entrenched in miracles
they're ordinary. Until a storyteller calls
them nonfiction science fiction.

Look long enough
anything's strange.
Mashed potatoes.
A zipper. Motel rooms.
Courage. The trance
from a flash of perception.
Inside-out sight.

Phenomenon: how unearthly
the Earth.

AN INTERGALACTIC SPACE GREETING

repurposed dialogue from Season 1, Episode 16

"Ahh-doo-nay-va-so barahghas."

Your encounter,
               Anecdotal data, trace evidence, self-delusion.
               Swamp gas, lightning, downright spooky.
atmospheric conditions can play tricks on you.

You're the only one I trust,
               A round-trip ticket taking an evasive route.
               A deep background heading West.
risked exposure come full circle.

A lie,
               So passionate, so blinding:
               the moon, half full.
hidden between two truths.

Means, "Hello, space brothers."
Means, "Just a tourist on a dangerous path."

DO YOU LIVE FOR BACH?

repurposed dialogue from Season 2, Episode 1

Four and a half billion years from now
                    when the sun engulfs Earth,

Voyager 1 will still travel across
                    swells in galactic latitude.

Little green men, white-bread swindles,
                    imaginings all locked inside

our small masses of tissue and fluid.

Ten million frequencies scanning;
                    we stepped out of our solar system.

Like galactic background noise,
                    like the "wow" signal

Bach's expression will still be out there

                    a hello

from the children of planet Earth.

Let's hear it again.

ABOUT THE AUTHOR

Amaris Feland Ketcham occupies her time with open space, white space, CMYK, flash nonfiction, long trails, f-stops, line breaks, and several Adobe programs running simultaneously. Her award-winning writing has appeared in *Creative Nonfiction*, *The Los Angeles Review*, *Prairie Schooner*, *Rattle*, the *Utne Reader*, and dozens of other venues. Her guidebook of New Mexico campgrounds is forthcoming from Menasha Ridge Press. Her previous book of poems, *A Poetic Inventory of the Sandia Mountains*, was published by Finishing Line Press in 2019. Her work with Poetic Routes has been adopted by the Albuquerque City Planning Department to use poetry as a means of understanding neighborhoods and community character throughout town. She has painted murals across Albuquerque, acted in a radio drama about the Badlands National Park, and taken students on multi-week camping trips along the Lewis and Clark Trail.

www.amarisketcham.com

CASA URRACA PRESS

We are a home for words that speak to the soul and stimulate thought. We publish daring, eloquent authors of poetry and creative nonfiction. And we offer workshops with our authors and other artists.

Every writer and every publisher has a slant. Ours tilts toward the richness of the high desert, where all are welcome who manage to find their way.

Proudly centered somewhere near Abiquiu, New Mexico.

For book orders and workshop registration, visit us at casaurracaltd.com.

@casaurracaltd
@casaurracaltd
casaurracaltd@gmail.com